Usborne

First Colouring Book
Dinosaurs

This book belongs to

- - - - - - - - - - - - - - - -

Giant dinosaurs

These huge dinosaurs were as big as a bus. They are called sauropods.

Tyrannosaurus rex

This big, scary dinosaur
was very fierce and ate
other dinosaurs.

Horned dinosaurs

These dinosaurs are called Triceratops.
They had three horns on their heads.

Under the sea

Some amazing sea creatures lived at the same time as the dinosaurs. The biggest one in this picture is a plesiosaur.

Spiky dinosaurs

These dinosaurs had spiky backs and tails.
They are called stegosaurs.

Baby dinosaurs

These hungry baby dinosaurs have just hatched out of their eggs. Their mother is bringing them some leaves to eat.

Giant wings

When the dinosaurs were alive, pterosaurs flew through the sky. Some were the size of small planes.

Lots of dinosaurs

Here are some different kinds
of dinosaurs to colour.